A Car Trip for Mole and Mouse

Harriet Ziefert
Pictures by David Prebenna

PUFFIN BOOKS

"This is a nice day," said Mole.
"Let's take a car trip."

"Okay," said Mouse.
"Let's take a trip.
Let's go to a flea market."

Mole got the car.
Mouse got the map.

"You drive the car," said Mouse.
"I will read the map.

And everything will be just fine."

Mole drove.

Mouse read the map.
And everything was just fine!

"I see a traffic circle,"
said Mole.
"What do I do?"

"Wait," said Mouse.
"I am looking at the map."

"Hurry!" said Mole.
"I don't know where to go."

Mole drove around and
around and around
the traffic circle.

At last Mouse said, "Take the road over the bridge."

"I don't like bridges," said Mole.

"Then take the tunnel
under the bridge,"
said Mouse.

"Good," said Mole.
"I like tunnels."

"It is dark in here,"
said Mouse.
"I can't read the map."

"That's okay," said Mole.
"I know all about tunnels."

Soon Mole and Mouse
were out of the tunnel.

"I'm hungry!" said Mole.

"I'll look for a place to stop," said Mouse.

Mole and Mouse stopped
at a stand.

Mole got ice cream.
Mouse got popcorn.

And everything was just fine!

"Get off here for the flea market," said Mouse.

Mole got off at the exit.
He went down the road and...

everything was not just fine!

"Don't worry!" said Mouse.
"I'll look at the map.
  We can go another way."

"No," said Mole.
"You take too long.
I'm going this way!"

"All right. All right," said Mouse.
"We can go your way."

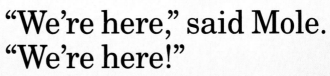

"I got us here," said Mouse.

Mole bought a desk.

And Mouse bought a chair.

And everything was just fine!

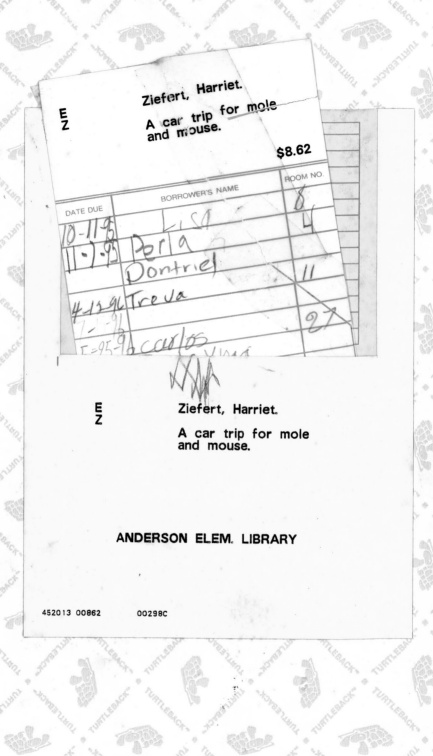

Ziefert, Harriet.

A car trip for mole
and mouse.

$8.62

E
Z

Ziefert, Harriet.

A car trip for mole
and mouse.

ANDERSON ELEM. LIBRARY